Troll Games

Books by Mary K. Whittington

CARMINA, COME DANCE!
TROLL GAMES

For Angie ~
Beware of trolls lurking
at St. Thomas More
(especially in 3rd grade!)

Mary K. Whittington 1994

To Wini Jaeger, with love and thanks
for her patience and support
M. K. W.

For Donna, Ann, Catherine, Marlene, and Tova
B. D.

Atheneum
Macmillan Publishing Company
866 Third Avenue, New York, NY 10022

Collier Macmillan Canada, Inc.
1200 Eglinton Avenue
Suite 200
Don Mills, Ontario M3C 3N1
First Edition
Printed in Hong Kong
10 9 8 7 6 5 4 3 2 1

Library of Congress Cataloging-in-Publication Data
Whittington, Mary K.
Troll games/Mary K. Whittington;
illustrated by Betsy Day.—1st ed.   p.   cm.
Summary: To escape the stew pot of the Four Frightful Troll
Brothers, T. Thomas Terwillig the Third tries to engage them in a series of
games intended to last until the sun rises to destroy them.
ISBN 0-689-31630-5
[1. Trolls—Fiction. 2. Games—Fiction.] I. Day, Betsy, ill.
II. Title.
PZ7.W6188Tr 1991 [E]—dc20
90-83 CIP AC

Troll Games

Mary K. Whittington
illustrated by Betsy Day

Mary K. Whittington (signature)

Atheneum 1991 New York

Collier Macmillan Canada
Toronto

Maxwell Macmillan International
Publishing Group
New York   Oxford   Singapore   Sydney

T. Thomas Terwillig the Third hurried up the mountain path. He should never have played that last game with the other children in the village. Before he'd known it, the sun had set, and now he was in danger. Somewhere between T. Thomas and home lurked the Four Frightful Troll Brothers, who came out of their troll hole every night at sunset to go hunting. If they caught him, he'd end up in their stew pot.

When he arrived at the first ridge, T. Thomas slipped into the shadow of an enormous boulder. It smelled of moldy mushrooms. Holding his nose, he peered across the valley. The moon shone so brightly, he could see every rock and shrub and shadow. On the next rise stood his cottage, a candle burning in each window. How he wished he were there by the fire, eating supper with Pap and Grandpappy.

At the foot of the rise lay the troll hole. Its door hung ajar, but the Four Frightful Troll Brothers were nowhere in sight. If they saw him, he might be able to outrun them. That's what he'd learned from the troll tales Pap and Grandpappy had told him.

The boulder cleared its throat. Before T. Thomas could leap away, a knobbly hand reached down and grabbed him.

"You're no boulder!" T. Thomas's knees trembled with fear, but he tried to sound brave. "You're a Frightful Troll Brother."

"Yep." The troll's jag-toothed grin nearly split his face in half. "And you are T. Thomas Terwillig the Third, and I've *got* you."

Bellowing all the way, he dragged poor T. Thomas down the side of the ridge into the valley. "Look what *I* got! Supper!"

Three more Frightful Troll Brothers rose from the edges of the path, where they had been pretending to be rocks.

The three-headed troll nabbed T. Thomas and pinched his arms and legs. "Yum. This here's the tasty, tender Terwillig."

"Let's see 'im," said the troll with one eye in the middle of his forehead. He thumped T. Thomas on the back. "He's ripe for eatin', he is."

The short troll poked his long nose at T. Thomas and sniffed. "Let's eat 'im now," he growled.

"Gotta cook 'im first." Jag Tooth threw T. Thomas over his shoulder and headed for the troll hole.

"Wait!" yelled T. Thomas. He took a deep breath. "You think I'm tender, but I'm really tough."

Three Heads scratched his middle one. "Stew pot'll fix that," he said.

"Maybe for ordinary people," said T. Thomas. "Not Terwilligs."

Jag Tooth put T. Thomas down. "How do we get you tenderer, Terwillig?" he asked.

T. Thomas knew he had to keep the brothers outside the troll hole till dawn. Something terrible happened to trolls if the sun struck them. "Exercise," he said, crossing his fingers. "We'll play games."

"Like what?" One Eye asked.

"Hide-and-seek, for starters," T. Thomas replied.

The Four Frightful Troll Brothers had never played hide-and-seek. T. Thomas explained the rules, slowly and patiently, again and again and again.

Finally, the trolls understood.

"I'm It first," yelled Long Nose.

"No, me," screeched Three Heads, and punched Long Nose.

"Me!" One Eye clouted Three Heads on his left chin.

"Wrong," roared Jag Tooth. "You hide. Me and Terwillig is It."

Grumbling, the others stumped away.

"You count, Terwillig," Jag Tooth demanded.

T. Thomas looked at the moon, high above. He counted slowly, but barely an hour passed before he reached one hundred. Maybe he could stretch the game another hour if he tried not to find the trolls.

"Don't worry, Terwillig," muttered Jag Tooth. "I knows where they all is. I been watchin' 'em. Game's over," he bellowed to his brothers.

"I'm starvin'," Long Nose said the minute he saw T. Thomas. "C'mon. Let's take 'im home."

"Wait!" yelled T. Thomas as Jag Tooth clutched him around the neck.

"What now?" Three Heads grumbled.

"I'm not tender yet," T. Thomas said. "We have to play another game."

"Like what?" One Eye said.

"King-of-the-hill," said T. Thomas.

The Four Frightful Troll Brothers had never played king-of-the-hill. T. Thomas explained the game until the moon was halfway down the western sky.

Finally, the trolls understood. They clumped off to a nearby mound.

"I'm King," yelled Long Nose, and climbed to the top.

"No. Me," screeched Three Heads, and bashed into Long Nose.

"Me!" One Eye charged up the mound and knocked his brothers flat.

"Wrong," roared Jag Tooth. He dragged T. Thomas over Long Nose, shoved One Eye out of the way, and stood on Three Heads. "Me and Terwillig is King of the hill. C'mon. Push us off. What're you waiting for?"

"Ooh, my head," groaned One Eye.

"Ow, my back," cried Three Heads.

"I hurts all over," moaned Long Nose.

Jag Tooth poked T. Thomas. "This is all your fault, Terwillig."
"Stew pot," said Long Nose.

"Wait!" T. Thomas yelled as Jag Tooth stuck him beneath one arm.

"What now?" Three Heads growled.

T. Thomas stared at the moon and willed it to move faster. "I'm sorry you got hurt," he said, "but the fact of the matter is, I'm still tough. One more game'll tenderize me for sure."

"Like what?" asked Long Nose.

T. Thomas's hands shook, so he shoved them in his pockets. "Tug-of-war," he said.

The Four Frightful Troll Brothers had never played tug-of-war. T. Thomas explained the game until the moon rested on the tips of the western mountains.

Finally, the trolls understood.

Now he had to get them up on the rise. Every morning, the sun shone there first before spilling into the valley. "Tell you

what," he said. "Let's play it in the squash-and-potato patch
near my cottage."

"Why?" Jag Tooth asked.

"Because the ground's soft, and we won't get hurt if we fall,"
said T. Thomas. "Besides, afterward, you can roll me right
down into your hole. I'll really be tender by then."

The trolls nodded. T. Thomas led them past the troll hole and up to the squash-and-potato patch. He glanced at the far horizon where the sky was beginning to lighten.

"It'll be Jag Tooth and Long Nose and me against Three Heads and One Eye," he said. "Now we need a rope."

"We ain't got one," Jag Tooth said.

"We don't need no rope," Long Nose growled. "We'll use Terwillig."

The trolls stopped to ponder that. Heart bumping, T. Thomas saw the first rays of the sun reaching into the sky. He began to edge toward the cottage.

"Grab 'im!" Long Nose screeched, and clamped a heavy hand around one of T. Thomas's arms.

"I want a leg!" yelled Three Heads, and grabbed one.

"Arm for me!" cried One Eye.

"Gimme that foot," Jag Tooth bellowed.

But as they started to pull, Long Nose let out a yell that shook the air. "The sun. The sun!"

The trolls dropped T. Thomas and froze. Their faces gleamed with sunshine. Scrambling away from their massive shapes, T. Thomas watched them turn gray. Cracks spread across their bodies. Four piles of stone settled slowly into the ground among the squash vines and potato plants.

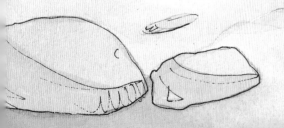

Later that week, T. Thomas told his story to the village
children and invited them to come play games on the rise.
There he showed them the Four Frightful Troll Brothers,
already half covered with squash vines.

T. Thomas and his friends climbed the troll stones. They
played hide-and-seek all over Jag Tooth and Three Heads,
and king-of-the-hill on One Eye and Long Nose. Afterward,
they played the best game of all, one they made up:
trolls-and-Terwillig.